ISBN 1-84135-186-5 (cased)
ISBN 1-84135-243-8 (limp)

First published 2003

Published by Award Publications Limited,
27 Longford Street, London NW1 3DZ

Printed in Malaysia

Barney's Surprising Spring-Clean

by Jackie Andrews
Illustrated by Lesley Smith

AWARD PUBLICATIONS LIMITED

Barney Bunny stood at his front door, sniffing the air.
“Mmm,” he said. “Spring is here.
Time to tidy the burrow.”

He went back inside and tidied
the cushions on his sofa.

Then he straightened his
teaspoons in the kitchen drawer.

He smoothed the quilt on his bed, then he hung his facecloth on its peg in the bathroom.

"There. All done. Now I can have some elevenses." (Or half-past-nineses, actually.)

But as Barney made his way to the kitchen, he suddenly had a horrible thought. The spare room!

Barney's spare room was like everyone else's attic. Except that you can't really have an attic in a burrow. He had all kinds of stuff there. Things he'd never used, but might need one day.

Gingerly, Barney put his head round the door.

Something fluffy and orange was wedged tight behind it.

Barney gave a tug.

It was a slipper in the shape of a carrot. They had been all the rage at one time.

"Well, that can go for a start!"

But as Barney was putting the slipper into his rubbish bin, Robin flew down.

"Morning, Barney," he said. "You're not throwing that slipper away, are you? It would make a nice nest, it would."

"Really? Would you like it?"

"Yes, please. Thanks, Barney!"

Robin flew off, delighted with the slipper. He returned a few minutes later, carrying a basket made from willow twigs.

"We thought you'd like this," he said.

"Oh. Thanks, Robin. That will be very useful," said Barney.

Barney pushed open the door to the spare room again. As he went inside, he tripped over something lumpy on the floor. He picked it up.

"It's that rucksack Great Aunt Beryl sent me for my birthday."

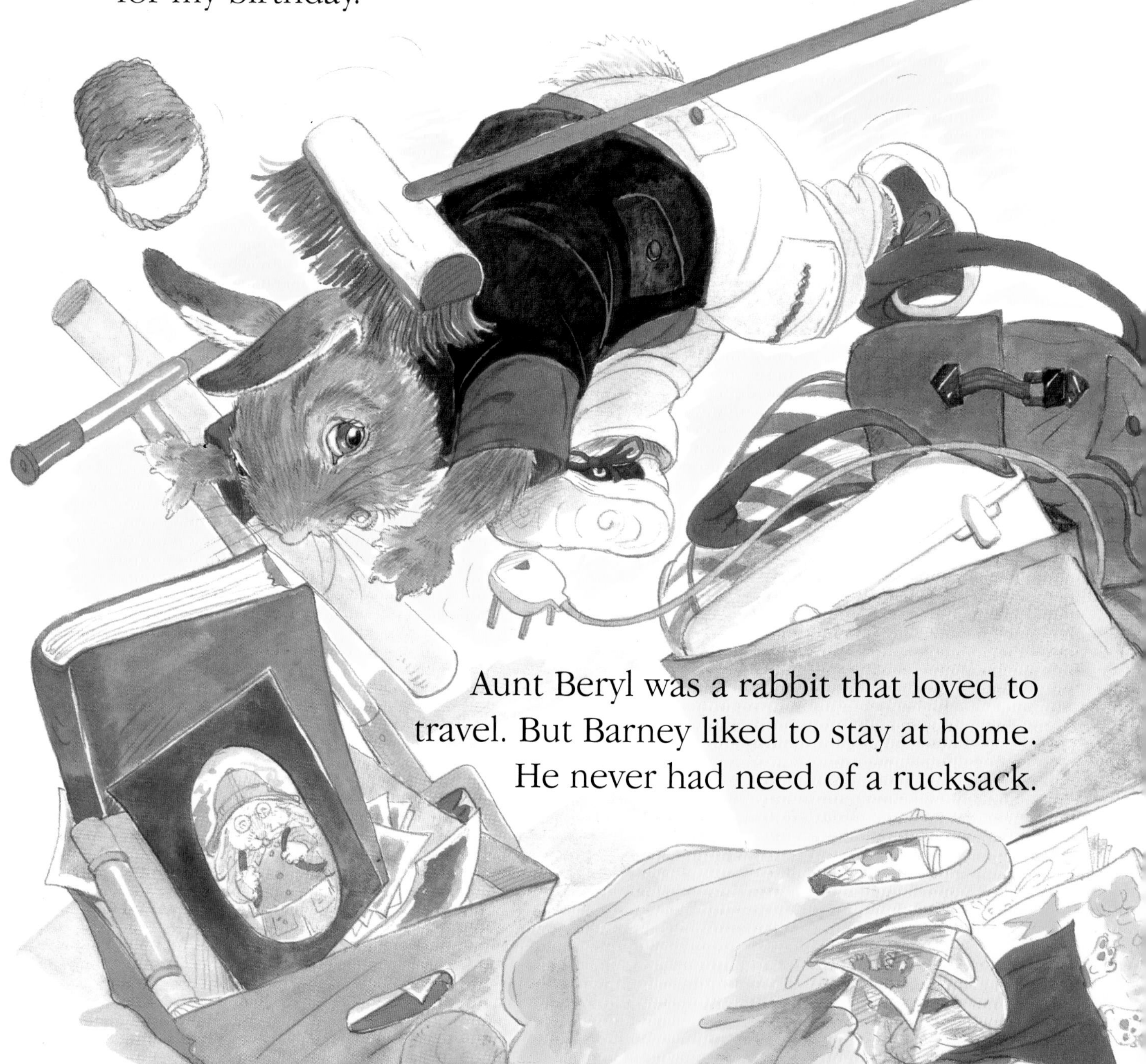

Aunt Beryl was a rabbit that loved to travel. But Barney liked to stay at home. He never had need of a rucksack.

So he put Robin's basket in a corner and took the rucksack out to the rubbish bin. Just then, Sally Squirrel went past.

"Good morning, Barney," said Sally. "You're not throwing that rucksack away, are you?"

"I've never used it," said Barney. "It's just cluttering up my burrow."

"That would be great for when I collect nuts for the winter," said Sally.

"Really? Would you like it?"

"Yes, please," said Sally. "Thanks, Barney."

Sally skipped away, delighted with the rucksack. She returned a few minutes later carrying a parasol.

"Here, I thought you'd like this, Barney. I don't need a parasol: I use my tail!"

"Oh. Thanks, Sally. That will be very useful," said Barney.

Barney put the parasol in the spare room. Then he remembered he hadn't had his elevenses, so he stopped for a cup of tea and a piece of cake.

"I wonder what I can get rid of next?" he thought.

Back in the spare room, Barney pulled out a wooden tea trolley.

"I certainly don't need this!"
He pushed the trolley into the garden.
Just then, Mrs Weasel came past with her six little weasels.
"Hello, Barney," she called. "You're not throwing that trolley away, are you?"

"Do you want it?" said Barney. "It's rather old."

"It's just what I need to carry my shopping. And the babies could sit on the top shelf!"

"Would you like it, Mrs Weasel?" asked Barney, with a small sigh.

"Oh, thank you!" Mrs Weasel filled the trolley with shopping and children and disappeared down the road.

A few minutes later, two of the weasel children scooted back, dragging a rolled-up rug between them.

"Ma says you're to have this. For the trolley!" they squeaked.

"Oh. Thanks," called Barney, after them. "Most useful!"

Barney propped the rug behind
the door of the spare room.

"Now then. What next?" he wondered.

With much shoving and heaving,
Barney pulled out a cardboard box.
"Electric breadmaker," he read.
"Well, I'll never use that!"

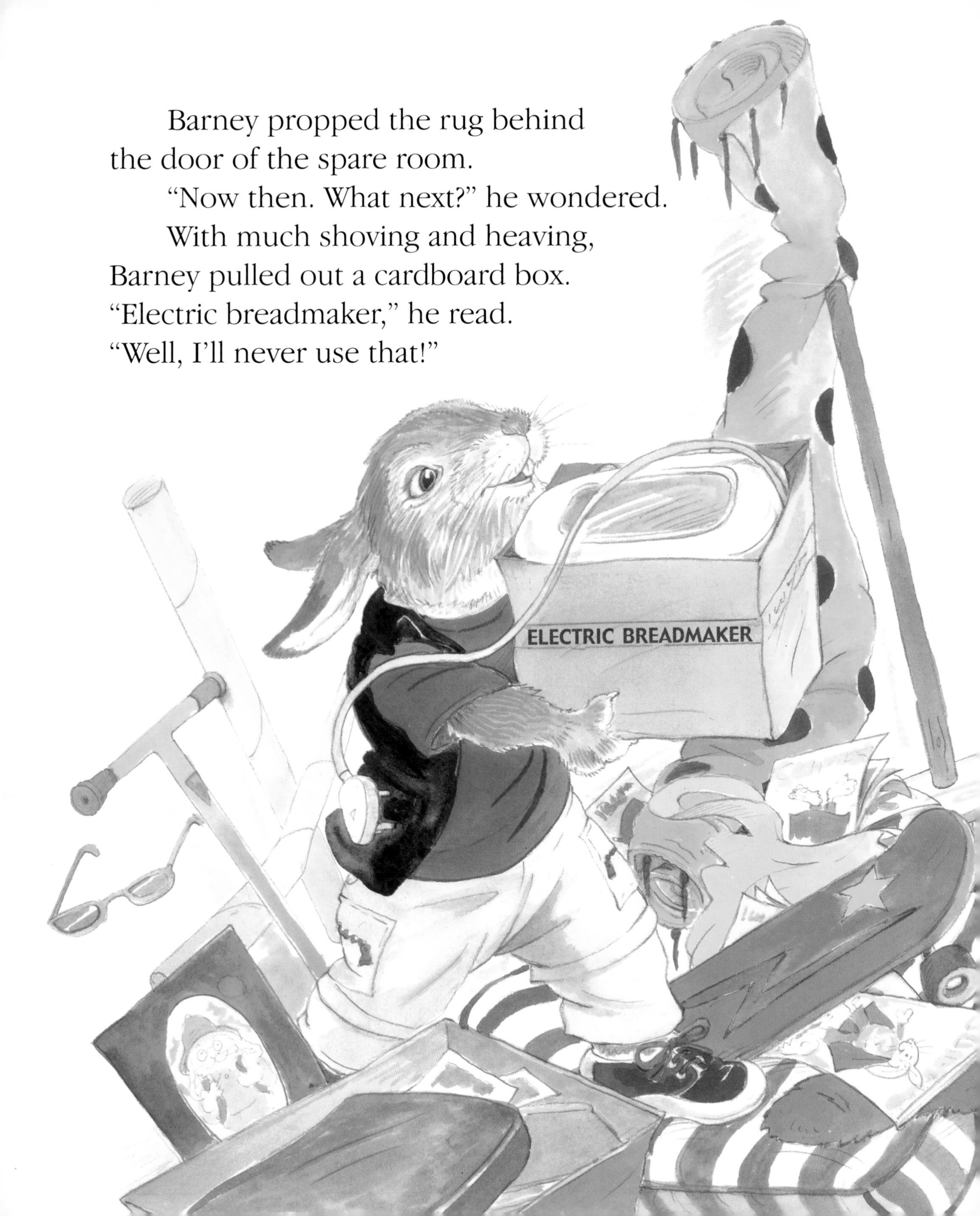

He took the box out to the rubbish bin just as Little Red Hen came by.

"Hello, Barney," she said. "What have you got there?"

"It's an electric breadmaker," said Barney. "I'm throwing it out."

"Oh, that's just what I need," said Little Red Hen eagerly.

"Really? Would you like it?"

"Thank you, Barney! Bread takes ages to make."

Little Red Hen fetched a wheelbarrow to carry the breadmaker.

"Here, Barney, I thought you'd like this," said Little Red Hen, and she gave Barney a large pot.

"Oh. Thanks," said Barney. "That will be useful."

He carried the pot into the spare room.

"Funny," he thought. "This room doesn't seem to be getting any emptier."

Then he spotted a box of old comics.

"No one could possibly want these," he said, and he took the box outside.

Barney lifted out one of the comics.
"*The Adventures of Super Bunny*.
Oh, wow! I loved this when I was little."
Barney sat down and began to read it again.

Just then his sister, Beattie, arrived with Barney's nieces and nephews.

"What are you doing, Uncle Barney?" they squeaked.

"Hello, Beattie. Hello Billy, Betty, Bramble and Bridget," said Barney. "I was just throwing out this box of old comics."

"Oh, can we throw them out, too?" shrieked the children.

"Of course," said Barney.

Beattie had brought a picnic. They all sat comfortably on the grass, eating sandwiches and looking through Barney's old comics.

"I used to love *Burrow Tales*," sighed Beattie.

The little rabbits were fascinated with them all. They had never been so quiet.

"Can we throw them out again when we come next time?" they asked.

"I suppose so," Barney said, laughing. "I shall just have to keep them for you."

After his visitors had gone home, Barney took the box of comics back into the spare room.

He just managed to shut the door.

“This spring-cleaning isn’t quite as easy as I thought,” said Barney at the end of day. “The spare room is still full of stuff, but at least most of it’s new stuff.”

He sipped his cocoa.

“But next year, I think I’ll just take all my rubbish to the dump before anyone sees it.”